H

 Symbols indicate the number of hazards on the page

Oops Hari!
by Tristan McGee
Edited by Sarah Cheeseman
Illustrated by Nicholas Halliday

First Published 2008. Reprinted 2011

A CIP catalogue record of this book is available from the British Library
ISBN 978-0-9559979-0-7
Printed in England

Mixed Sources
Product group from well-managed forests and other controlled sources
www.fsc.org Cert no. TT-COC-002495
© 1996 Forest Stewardship Council
FSC

CarbonNeutral® printing company

Tristan McGee

Afternoon
Nap
HARI CRAYON
HARI CRAYON
CRAYON

Hari was lying on the sofa
under his favourite blanket having an afternoon
nap, when Moe started jumping up and down on
his tummy.

"Wake up, Hari!" he shouted.
"We'll be late meeting our friends at the beach."

Hari jumped up and ran into the kitchen
for his glass of cold milk and chocolate cookies.

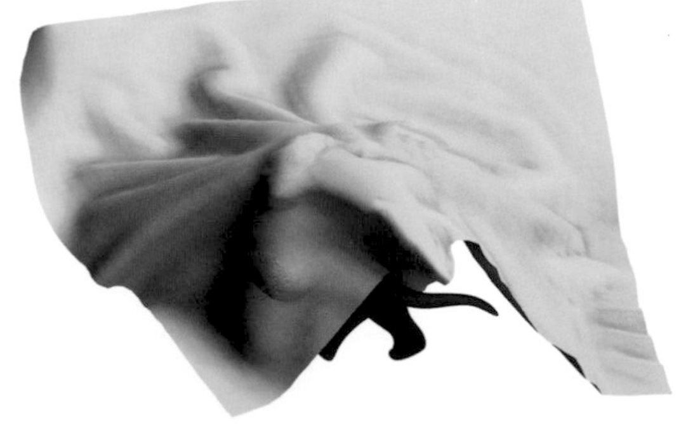

"I need my bicycle helmet!" shouted Hari.
"Where's my bicycle helmet?"

"You're wearing it!" said Moe from under Hari's blanket, but Hari wasn't listening.

Hari climbed up onto his chair, put his feet against the table and drank his milk.

"Careful, Hari," warned Moe. *"Don't lean baaaaack!"*

'CRASH!' Hari fell back off his chair and bumped his head on the floor, with the milk spilling everywhere.

Moe was thrown through the air and straight out of the kitchen door...

FIRST AID
Oops Hari!

...and bounced on a toy Hari had left on the stairs. Hari was always forgetting to put his toys away in the toy box after playing with them.

The startled toy watched as Hari rushed past them on his way up to the bathroom.

"I'm going to wash the milk off!" he shouted. *"And then we must rush to meet our friends at the beach!"*

"Hold onto the handrail, Hari!" called Moe. *"And don't run on the stairs!"*

In the bathroom, Hari dragged his stool over to the sink and climbed onto it. He turned on the taps and splashed water everywhere, making a large puddle on the floor.

"Be careful, Hari! The water is very hot," warned Moe. *"Always run the cold water first!"*

Sleeping Pills
32 Pills
PARACETAMOL
PARACETAMOL

After washing off the milk, Hari got down from his stool and headed for the door.

"Please mop up before you go," said Moe, *"but don't use the bathmat... Oh, Hari!"*

"Let's go!" shouted Hari.

As he ran along the corridor towards the stairs,
Moe shouted, *"Don't run down the stairs, it's very dangerous!"*

"I need my bicycle helmet," shouted Hari.
"Where's my bicycle helmet?"

But before Moe could tell him,
Hari tripped over the toy on the stairs.

Oops Hari!

Hari, Moe and the toy **flewww** through the air and landed in a heap at the bottom of the stairs.

Hari and Moe picked themselves up and ran out into the garden.

"I can't ride my new bike without my helmet!" cried Hari, as they headed for the garden gate.

"I wish I knew where my bicycle helmet was!"

"Wait!" cried Moe, as Hari opened the gate and ran into the road.

"Always stop, look and listen before you cross the road, even at a zebra crossing."

Oops Hari!

As soon as Hari got to the beach he put on his bright red armbands and went for a swim in the sea.

He paddled about, spraying water from his trunk.

"Hari," cried Moe. *"You forgot to put on your sun cream."*

Back on the beach, Hari met up with his friends.

"We've all been waiting for you, Hari," they said. *"Why didn't you bring your bike?"*

"I couldn't find my bicycle helmet," Hari replied.

His friends all pointed to his head.

"You're wearing it, Hari!" they laughed.

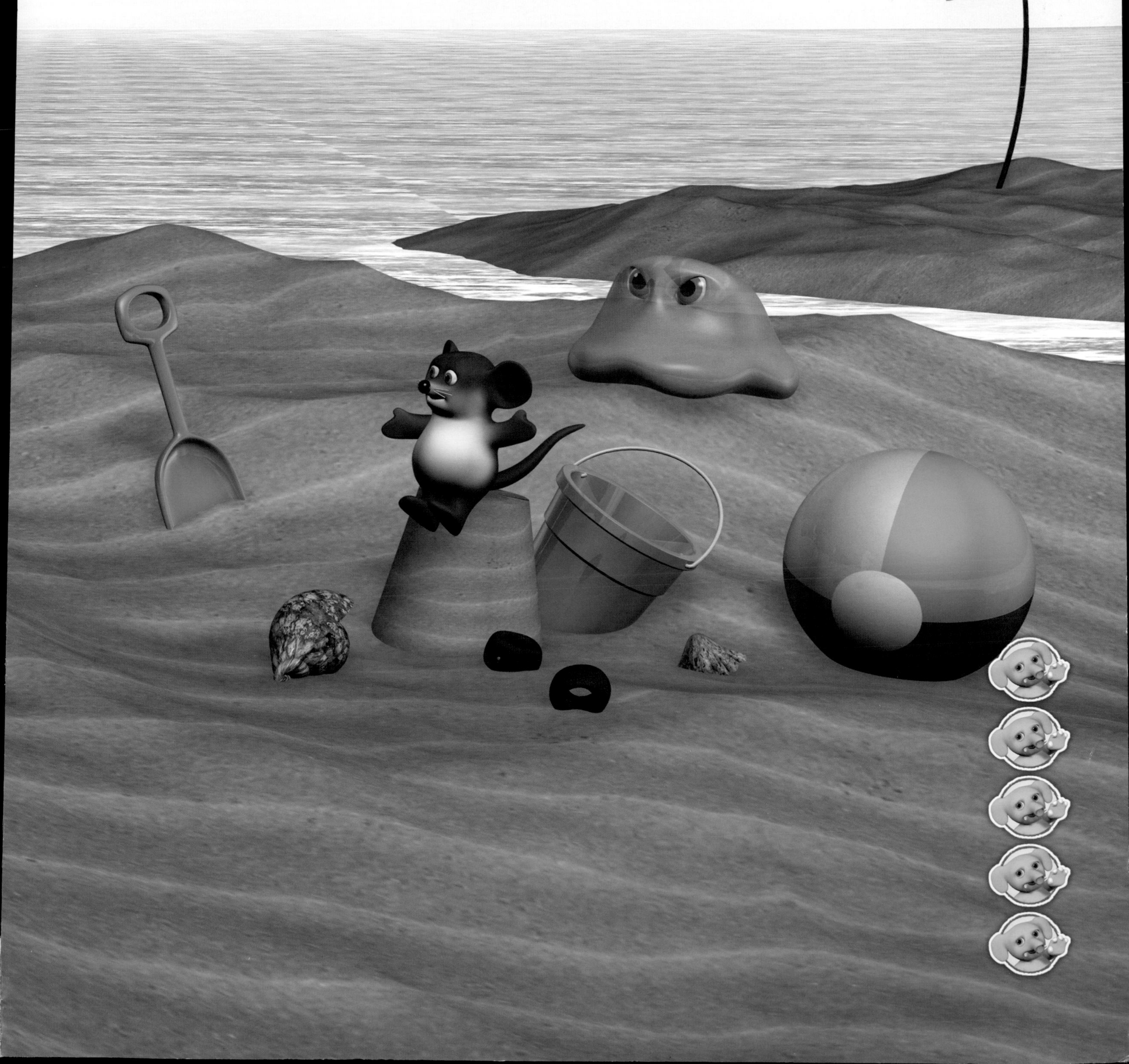

"Silly me! I'll go and get my bike,"
sang Hari, as he skipped back
across the soft golden sand.

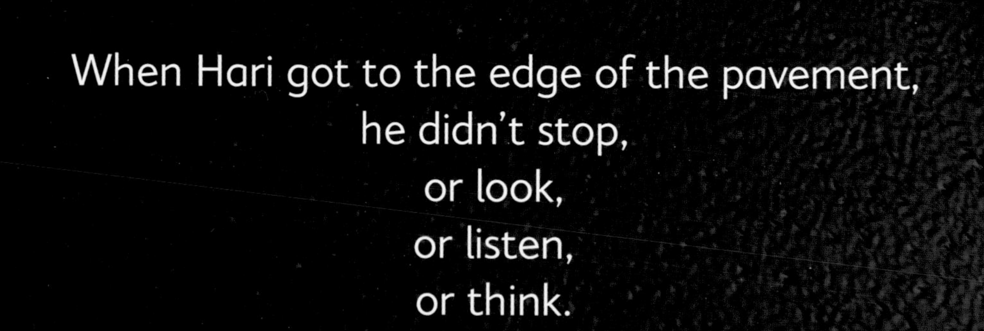

When Hari got to the edge of the pavement,
he didn't stop,
or look,
or listen,
or think.

Instead, he ran straight into the middle of the road.

"Don't run out between parked cars!" shouted Moe, as an angry red car screeched to a stop.

Hari was startled and ran into the road sign.

'Ouch!' cried Hari.

'Ouch!' cried Moe.

'Ouch!' cried the sign.

30
H
SCREECH
Oops
Hari!

Safely back home, Hari and Moe rested on the sofa. Hari put a plaster on Moe's head and one on his trunk.

"I wish I had a bicycle helmet," said Moe.

Oops Moe!

To Moe
with love
FROM
Hari
x

There are three books currently available in the Oops Hari! series for you to enjoy

When Hari gets up late from his nap, he has to rush to meet his friends, but he can't find his bicycle helmet. Moe is trying to tell him where it is, but Hari just isn't listening!

ISBN 978-0-9559979-0-7

When Sting the Wasp flies into Hari's bedroom on a lazy Saturday morning, Max the Dog begins a chase that leads them all over the house and garden. Moe tries to warn Max about annoying Sting, but Max just isn't listening!

ISBN 978-0-9559979-4-5

When Pinch the Crab is found in his little rock pool on a sunny day at the beach, Hari and Max the Dog begin a chase that leads them along the beach and the pier to the cliff bottom. Moe tries to warn them about annoying Pinch, but they just aren't listening. When Hari and his friends go for a swim, Pinch has other ideas!

ISBN 978-0-9559979-6-9